Plains Cree/English edition

kimotinâniwiw itwêwina

Stolen Words

omasinahikêw Melanie Florence

otâpasinahikêw Gabrielle Grimard

Dolores Sand êkwa Gayle Weenie kî-nêhiyawastâwak

Written by Melanie Florence

Illustrated by Gabrielle Grimard

Translated by Dolores Sand and Gayle Weenie

Second Story Press

For Josh, Taylor, and Chris.
And for my grandfather.
—M.F.

To my family.
—G.G.

Library and Archives Canada Cataloguing in Publication

Title: kimotinâniwiw itwêwina / omasinahikêw Melanie Florence ; otâpasinahikêw Gabrielle Grimard ; Dolores Sand êkwa Gayle Weenie kî-nêhiyawastâwak = Stolen words / written by Melanie Florence ; illustrated by Gabrielle Grimard ; translated by Dolores Sand and Gayle Weenie.

Other titles: Stolen words

Names: Florence, Melanie, author. | Grimard, Gabrielle, illustrator. | Sand, Dolores Greyeyes, translator. | Weenie, Gayle, translator. | Container of (work): Florence, Melanie. Stolen words. | Container of (expression): Florence, Melanie. Stolen words. Cree.

Description: Text in Cree translation and in original English.

Identifiers: Canadiana 20190090979 | ISBN 9781772601015 (softcover)

Subjects: CSH: Native peoples—Canada—Residential schools—Juvenile fiction.

Classification: LCC 2019 | LCC PS8611.L668 S7612 2019 | DDC jC813/.6—dc23

Translation copyright © 2019 Dolores Sand and Gayle Weenie
Text copyright © 2017 Melanie Florence
Illustrations copyright © 2017 Gabrielle Grimard

Editor/art director Kathryn Cole
Design by Melissa Kaita

Printed and bound in China

Special thanks to Dr Jean Okimâsis, honorary founder, Cree Literacy Network, and to Arok Wolvengrey and Solomon Ratt, Professors of Indigenous Languages, Arts and Cultures, First Nations University of Canada. And to Arden Ogg, Director of the Cree Literacy Network.

Second Story Press gratefully acknowledges the support of the Ontario Arts Council and the Canada Council for the Arts for our publishing program. We acknowledge the financial support of the Government of Canada through the Canada Book Fund.

ONTARIO ARTS COUNCIL
CONSEIL DES ARTS DE L'ONTARIO
an Ontario government agency
un organisme du gouvernement de l'Ontario

Canada Council   Conseil des arts
for the Arts   du Canada

Funded by the   Financé par le
Government   gouvernement
of Canada   du Canada

Canada

Published by
Second Story Press
20 Maud Street, Suite 401
Toronto, Ontario, Canada
M5V 2M5
www.secondstorypress.ca

nêhiyawastâwin ohci

anima nêhiyawastâwin kimotinâniwiw itwêwina ohci kî-tôtamwak Dolores Sand êkwa Gayle Weenie paskwâwi-nêhiyawêwin ê-pîkiskwêcik. ê-isi-nîsicik Saskatchewan ohci, Dolores wiya maskêko-sâkahikanihk ohci êkwa Gayle wiya nakiwacîhk ohci.

About the Translation

The translation of *Stolen Words* was done by Plains Cree language speakers Dolores Sand and Gayle Weenie. Both from Saskatchewan, Dolores is from Muskeg Lake Cree Nation and Gayle Weenie is from Sweetgrass First Nation.

kî-pê-kîwêw anohc kiskinwahamâtowikamikohk ohci.
ê-kwâskohcisit êkwa ê-nîmihicosit. ê-kâmwâci-nikamosit.
miciminam pawâtam-ayapiy ê-kî-osîhtât konita kîkwâsa ohci.
pîminâhkwânisa, iyinito-mîkisak êkwa mîkwanisak ê-wâsêsicik
nanâtohk ê-isinâkosicik.
ê-wâsêyâyiki ocapihkânisa tâpiskôc ê-nîmihito-ihtât otihtimanihk.
ê-wîci-waskawîmikot.
kaskitêwâyiwa tâpiskôc kâhkâkiw otahtahkwan.

She came home from school today.
Skipping and dancing. Humming a song under her breath.
Clutching a dream catcher she had made from odds and ends.
Bits of string. Plastic beads. And brightly colored feathers.
Her glossy braids danced against her shoulders.
Swaying with her. Black as a raven's wing.

"mosôm," kakwêcimêw, ê-sakicihcênât,
ê-wâsakâmêpayihot capasis ospitoniyiw mwayês
ê-pakicihcênât kîhtwâm.
"tânisi kititwân *grandfather* ê-nêhiyawêyan?"
pôni-yêhyêyiwa aciyaw omosôma.
tâpiskôc nipahi-kinwêsk awiyak kâ-têpakohpopiponêt.

Grandpa, she asked, clutching his hand,
spinning under his arm before dropping it again.
How do you say grandfather in Cree?
He stopped breathing for a moment.
A lifetime to a seven year old.

kitâpamêw ê-pîkiskâcinâkosit.

"namôya nikiskisin," isi-naskwêwasimêw.

"nikî-wanihtân nititwêwina kayâs."

mâmaskâtam isinâkosiw.

"nimosôm, tânisi ê-isi-wanihtâyan itwêwina," kakwêcimêw.

"nikî-maskamikwak," naskwêwasimêw.

aciyaw mâmitonêyihtam.

"tânitê ê-kî-itohtatâcik?" kâ-kakwêcihkêmot.

He looked down at her sadly.

I don't remember, he answered.

I lost my words a long time ago.

A frown clouded her face.

How do you lose words, Grandpa? she asked.

They took them away, he answered.

She thought for a moment.

Where did they take them? she asked.

"itê kâ-kî-itohtahikoyâhkik," itwêw.

"wâhyaw ohci nîkinâhk, wâhyaw pâhpiwinihk ohci êkwa papêyâhtik itwêwina ohci.

wâhyaw nikâwînânak ohci kâ-mawîhkâtikoyâhkik."

sakicihcênam owâh-wâkicihcîyiw.

"awîna kâ-kî-sipwêhtahisk, mosôm?" papêyâhtik kakwêcimêw.

"nâpêwak êkwa iskwêwak ê-kaskitêwisihocik.

ê-pîkiskwâtikoyâhkik itwêwina ohci êkâ ê-kî-nisitohtamâhk," naskwêwasimêw.

ati-takohtêwak wîkiwâhk êkwa nîswapiwak tahkoskâcikanihk.

Where they took all of us, he said.
Away from home. Away from laughter and soft words.
Away from our mothers who cried for us.
She reached for his gnarled hand.
Who took you away, Grandpa? she asked quietly.
Men and women dressed in black.
Talking to us with words we did not know, he answered.
They reached home and sat on the stairs together.

"tânitê kâ-kî-itohtahiskik, mosôm?" kakwêcimêw.

"ohpimê kiskinwahamâtowikamikohk ê-tahkastêk êkwa ê-pîkiskâcihk,
itê wâpiski-mihkwâkana ê-kisiwinâkwahki ê-kisiwi-pîkiskwêcik
êkwa ê-ohpiniskêyicik mâna ispîhk kâ-âpacihtâyâhk
nititwêwininâna," naskwêwasimêw.

"kî-otinamwak nititwêwininâna êkwa kî-kikâpiskahamwak ohpimê,
ê-kî-kitimahikoyâhkik piyisk ka-wanikiskisiyâhk
isko ka-itihtâkosiyâhk tâpiskôc wiyawâw."

Where did they take you, Grandpa? she asked.
Away to a school that was cold and lonely,
where angry white faces raised their voices and their hands
when we used our words, he answered.
They took our words and locked them away,
punished us until we forgot them,
until we sounded like them.

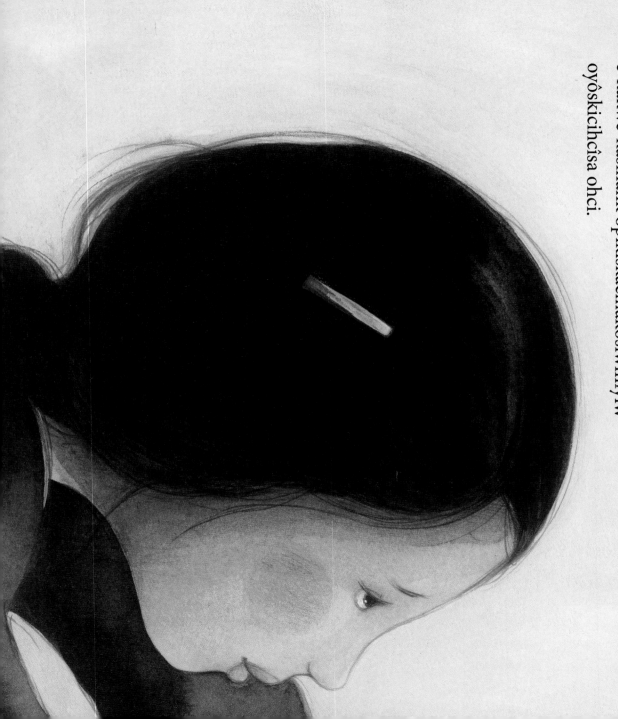

"ê-wîsakihtâkwahki mîna ê-kâsisihtâkwahki itwêwina,
misi-pîtos iyikohk kâ-miyohtâkwahki kiyânaw."
sâminam osikwêhkwêwiniyihk.
ê-kakwê-kâsîhahk opîkiskâcinâkosiwiniyiw
oyôskicihcîsa ohci.

Harsh sharp words.
So different from the sound of our beautiful ones.
She touched his weathered face.
Tried to wipe the sadness away
with her soft hands.

kitâpahtam anima kâ-kî-osîhtât êwakw ânima miyêw
pawâtam-ayapiy onipêwikamikohk ohci kâ-kî-osîhtât.
"ôtina ôma, mosôm," itêw.
"ahpô êtikwê ka-wîcihikon ka-miskaman kititwêwina kîhtwâm."
pâhpihkwêstawêw. ôsisima.
sâminam okanâci-wihkwâkaniyiw.
mihkwâkan êkâ wîhkâc kâ-ohci-kiskêyihtahk kisiwi-itwêwina.
ahpô ka-ohpiniskêyîstâkot awiya.
pâhpisiw êkwa ocêmêw ostikwâniyihk.

She looked down at her lap and handed him
the dream catcher that she had made for her room.
You take this Grandpa, she said.
Maybe it will help you find your words again.
He smiled at her. His granddaughter.
And touched her innocent face.
A face that had never known hard words.
Or raised hands.
He smiled and kissed her head.

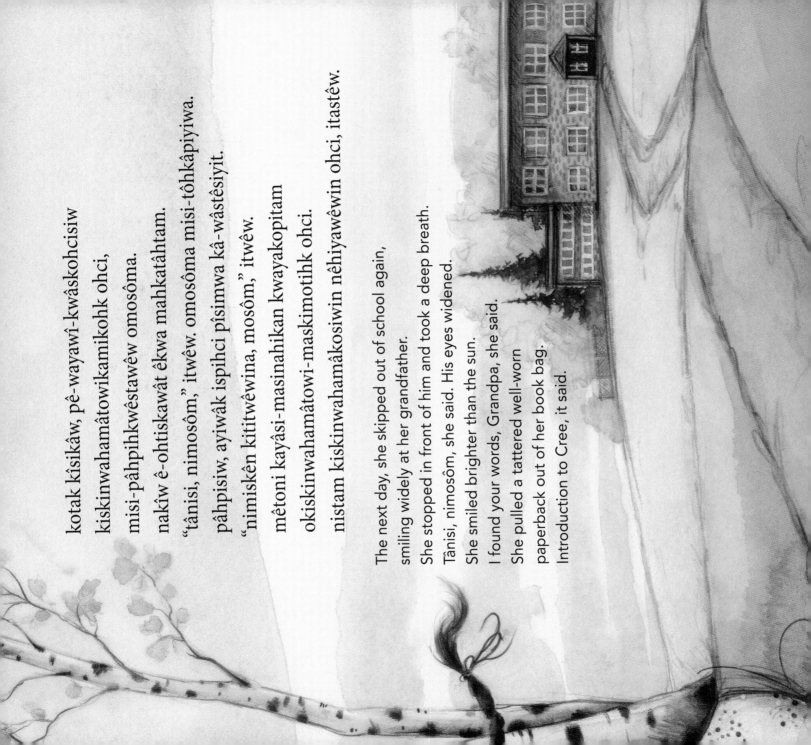

kotak kîsikâw, pê-wayawî-kwâskohcisiw
kiskinwahamâtowikamikohk ohci,
misi-pâhpihkwêstawêw omosôma.
nakîw ê-ohtiskawât êkwa mahkatâhtam.
"tânisi, nimosôm," itwêw. omosôma misi-tôhkâpiyiwa.
pâhpisiw, ayiwâk ispihci pîsimwa kâ-wâstêsiyit.
"nimiskên kititwêwina, mosôm," itwêw.
mêtoni kayâsi-masinahikan kwayakopitam
okiskinwahamâtowi-maskimotihk ohci.
nistam kiskinwahamâkosiwin nêhiyawêwin ohci, itastêw.

The next day, she skipped out of school again,
smiling widely at her grandfather.
She stopped in front of him and took a deep breath.
Tânisi, nimosôm, she said. His eyes widened.
She smiled brighter than the sun.
I found your words, Grandpa, she said.
She pulled a tattered well-worn
paperback out of her book bag.
Introduction to Cree, it said.

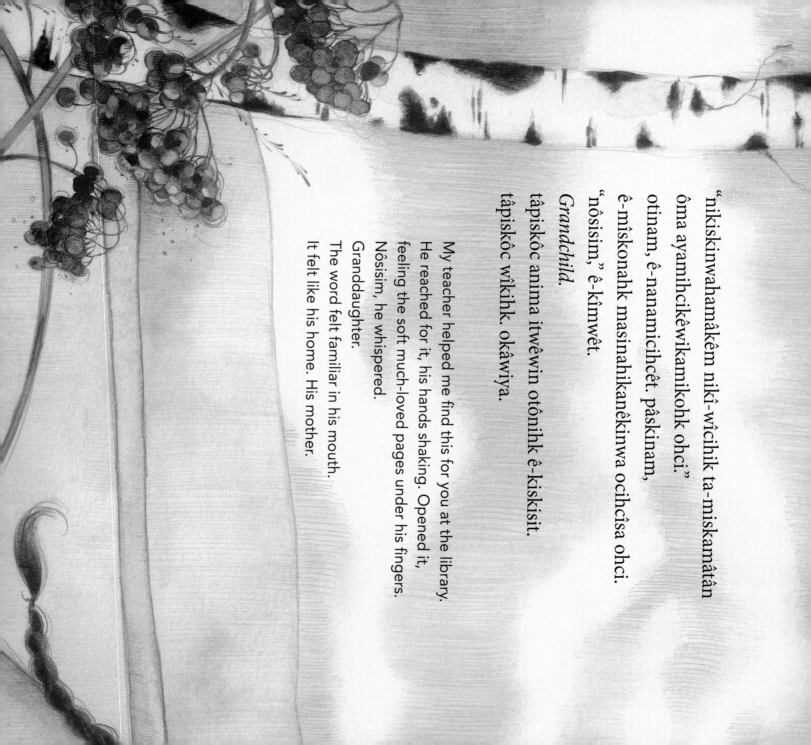

"nikiskinwahamâkêm nikî-wîcihik ta-miskamâtân
ôma ayamihcikêwikamikohk ohci."
otinam, ê-nanamicihcêt. pâskinam,
ê-mîskonahk masinahikanêkinwa ocihcîsa ohci.
"nôsisim," ê-kîmwêt.
Grandchild.
tâpiskôc anima itwêwin otônihk ê-kiskisit.
tâpiskôc wîkihk. okâwiya.

My teacher helped me find this for you at the library.
He reached for it, his hands shaking. Opened it,
feeling the soft much-loved pages under his fingers.
Nôsisim, he whispered.
Granddaughter.
The word felt familiar in his mouth.
It felt like his home. His mother.

papêyâhtik kî-pâskinam masinahikanêkinwa.
Book. masinahikan.
kotak pâskinam. itwêwin mîna kotak itwêwin.
Language. pîkiskwêwin. otitwêwina. mêtoni mihcêt
pâski-masinahikanêkinwa.
kitâpamêw ôsisima, wiya tipiyaw ôsisima.
kinanâskomitin. "ay-hay, tîniki," itwêw.

He turned the pages of the book carefully.
Masinahikan. Book. He turned another. Word after word.
Pîkiskwêwin. Language. His words. Pages and pages of them.
He looked at his granddaughter, ôsisima.
Thank you. Tîniki, he said.

"ka-kî-ayamihtamawin cî?" isi-kakwêcimêw.
sakicihcênêw ê-ati-kîwêhtahât.
"ka-kî-kiskinwahamawin cî kititwêwina?"
nîmihitômakaniyiw otêh ê-nanamiskwêyit,
wâskikanihk ê-ma-miciminahk omasinahikan.

Will you read to me? she asked,
taking his hand in hers and leading him home.
Will you teach me your words?
His heart danced as he nodded,
holding the book against his chest.

English Translation and Pronunciation of the Cree Words Found in the Story

The six Cree words in this story are the same in all three of the major western Cree dialects: Plains Cree (y-dialect, also called nêhiyawêwin), Swampy Cree (n-dialect, also called ininîmowin), and Woodlands Cree (th-dialect, also called nîhithowîwin).

tânisi [TAHN-sih] : hello

tânisi is the word most commonly used in greeting. We usually translate it as hello. tânisi is also the question word how. While we think hello in English, Cree is also asking, How are you?

nimosôm [NIHmusoom] : my grandfather

nimosôm means my grandfather. Your grandfather is kimosôm. His or her grandfather is omosôma. Cree families speaking English often shorten the word to mosôm.

nôsisim [NOHS-sim] : my grandchild

nôsisim literally means my grandchild. In this book, nôsisim is translated as my granddaughter. Without the pictures and context, it could also be translated as my grandson. Cree doesn't actually have separate words for granddaughter or grandson. And in Cree culture, nôsisim is an affectionate way for a Cree elder to address a young person, whether they are related or not. ôsisima [o-SIS-ima] is the form for his or her grandchild.

masinahikan [mussih-NUH-eegun] : book

masinahikan can also be translated into English as letter, report, paper, document, drawing, or magazine—all depending on context.

pîkiskwêwin [peeKISS-kwaywin] : language

pîkiskwêwin is used in this book to mean language. It too, can be translated into several different English words including: expression or phrase; speech, talk, or conversation; lecture; voice.

tîniki [TEEN-key] : thank-you

tîniki is one of several ways people say thank you in Cree. This form seems to have been borrowed from English. Other informal words used for thanks include hay-hay (mostly in Alberta); or êkosi meaning that's good, that's enough (mostly in Manitoba).

A more detailed guide for this book can be found at
www.secondstorypress.ca/kids/stolen-words
This guide is provided by the Cree Literacy Network:
director of the Cree Literacy Network: www.creeliteracy.org

SRO: y

Cree Literacy Network

omasinahikêw ohci

Melanie Florence, âpihtawikosisân, nêhiyaw êkwa Scottish, kihc-âyiwikosiw omasinahikêwin ohci. kî-masinaham kimotinâniwiw itwêwina ta-kistêyimât omosôma, ê-kî-sâkihât kâ-awâsisîwit. namôya wîhkâc ohci-ispayiw ta-pîkiskwâtât onêhiyâwiwiniyiw ohci, êkosi kî-masinaham ôma âcimowin nanâtawihowin ê-pakosêyihtamawât. Melanie wîkiw Toronto asici onâpêma êkwa nîso otawâsimisa.

About the Author

Melanie Florence is an award-winning writer of Cree/Scottish heritage. She wrote *Stolen Words* in honor of her grandfather, whom she was close to as a child. Melanie never had the chance to speak to him about his Cree heritage, and this story is about the healing relationship she wishes she had been able to have with him. Melanie lives with her husband and two children in Toronto.

otâpasinahikêw ohci

Gabrielle Grimard âpacihtâw nanâtohk âpacihcikana kâ-tâpasinahikêstahk masinahikan ohci, mâka ê-mâwaci-miywêyihtahk itasinâstêwina. kî-tâpasinaham mihcêt masinahikana. êkwa kî-otinâw tahtwâw ka-mawinahikêt ta-paskiyâkêt otahikêwin. Gabrielle wîkiw cîki Sherbrooke, Quebec.

About the Illustrator

Gabrielle Grimard uses various media to create the illustrations for a book, but her favorite aspect will always be color. She has illustrated dozens of books and has been nominated for several awards. Gabrielle lives near Sherbrooke, Quebec.